IF FLIRTS

COULD KILL

IF FLIRTS

COULD KILL

JOEY YOUNG

First edition, 2016

ISBN-13: 978-0692700518

Dedicated to Cora.

Prologue

MIA Rojas would have made a great secret agent if only she wasn't such a shameless flirt. It's kind of hard to catch bad guys when you have the hots for them.

She was in the midst of her freshman year at Ingleton Academy in San Diego, California. Ingleton was a place where the top secret agents of tomorrow were crafted. The college was prestigious in its own right—an elite institution in where you had to know someone high on the food chain even to be considered for admission. Even then, you could only become "transcripted" into the Black Penguins if you had Penguin in your blood at birth.

Mia's father was a Black Penguin. As was her big sister, Angelina—who everyone called Angel. This nickname infuriated Mia; a constant reminder of how perfect her big sister was and how Mia, by comparison, was a little devil child.

Chapter 1

MIA giggled and hiccupped her way over to her dorm room in Pistachio Hall. Room 346; her nest of spent whiskey bottles, used condom wrappers, and other contraband.

As she approached her door, she held her keys in one hand and Jason's tough-guy arm in the other. But she couldn't get her eyes to focus, and she dropped the keys onto the ground by her feet.

"Do you have a master plan for world domination?" she asked him, sliding a finger down his chest.

He bent down and picked up the keys. "Are you going to try and stop me?"

"You know I'm not going to let you get away with it, Jason. I'm Agent Sparrow. I always get my man."

He grinned, then turned the key in the hole and opened the door. "You ain't no agent, girl. You're just a freshman." He kissed her lavishly on the neck, then said, in a very matter-of-fact voice, "This week I'm going to kill the President. What do you think about *that*?"

She twirled a strand of her hair around her finger. "You're so funny!"

Before they even got through the doorway, Jason pulled her top off and threw it into a nearby garbage can. "You won't be needing *that* anymore."

Jason went for her shorts next. He unbuttoned them and they dropped to her ankles. She kicked them drunkenly against the dorm room wall and toppled backwards onto her bed.

"Oh, Jason!" She squirmed and wriggled, then asked the rhetorical question: "Are you going to fuck me?"

The door flew open just then. A stern-looking woman in a sleek black suit with an appalled look on her face shouted, "Private Sparrow!"

Mia, who had at this point been stripped of all but her underwear, sprang to her feet. "It's not what it looks like, Captain Anderson!"

"I've had enough of this!" She stomped a foot dramatically on the floor. "Fornication on school grounds, in the dorms no less, is cause for immediate expulsion, Sparrow!"

"Let me explain!" She fumbled with her thoughts, casting Jason a glance, hoping he might have a story in mind and help her out. But he didn't. He just sat there, a big dumb deer-in-headlights look on his face.

"And who is this *thug*?" Anderson asked. "Do you even know his name?"

"Captain! This is Luis Perez. He's my . . . My . . ."

Think, Mia.

"My doctor," she finally stammered, covering herself with a blanket. "And I wanted to have a physical done. I thought I found a lump."

"You expect me to believe that, Private Sparrow?"

Jason got up and held out a hand to Anderson. "Luis Perez. Doctor of Medicine." It almost sounded convincing.

The hand stayed there, hovering awkwardly in mid-air. "You don't look old enough to be a doctor to me. You licensed to practice medicine?" she asked him.

Before he could respond, Mia answered on his behalf. "It's a Peruvian thing," she interjected. "You can practice after four years. I only do Peruvian doctors." Then, as an afterthought, she added, "It's my religion."

"Is that so?" Anderson replied. Mia knew that Anderson was a devout Catholic, so Mia figured if she played the religious freedom card she might stand a chance.

"No members of the opposite gender in the dorms. Why didn't you get a female doctor?" Anderson asked.

"There are none, not in Peru," Mia said. "Women have no rights over there."

Anderson reluctantly shook Jason's hand. Never mind that he didn't look a bit Peruvian, and with tattoos scribbled all over his neck, he certainly didn't look like a doctor.

"Well, Dr. Perez, if you wish to conduct an exam on school grounds, you need to obtain permission from the Dean first."

"I apologize. I didn't know," Jason said, buttoning his shirt.

"Hey, wait a minute . . ." Anderson said. Her mouth twisted into a sneer. "You're that guy on the news! The one who robbed Six Flags!"

Jason withdrew a gun from underneath his shirt and stuck it in Anderson's face. "You never saw me. You got that?" Anderson stood immobile at the doorway, speechless and with a terrified look in her eyes.

Jason pushed past her and scampered down the hall. Then he was gone.

Anderson turned to Mia and scowled. "Get dressed, Private! You are in so much trouble!" She turned on her heel and started to march away.

Mia, meanwhile, struggled to put her clothes back on, which was a challenge due to her state of inebriation. Finally, with her shorts on backwards and a jacket hoodie for cover, she caught up with Anderson in the hallway.

"Captain! Please!" Mia grabbed her by the shoulder. "Don't tell the Dean! You know what my dad will do to me if I get expelled?"

Anderson pulled away from her. "*No.* You listen to me, Private Sparrow. This is the last straw. Ever since you first arrived in this institution, it's been the same thing. You always have to test the limits, don't you, Sparrow? When are you going to *grow up*?"

"I promise, I'll behave. I won't do it again."

"You've violated every rule in the Ingleton handbook. Enough is enough."

"Give me one more chance," Mia begged. Some remote, seldom visited corner of her brain that was devoted to logic told her that this time could be the last for her. It had been like this with Anderson all semester, and she hadn't even had her midterms yet.

"Sparrow, maybe this is a good thing. This school is not a good fit for you. Maybe it's time to think about a different line of work."

"What?"

"Maybe being a secret agent just isn't your calling," Anderson suggested.

Mia was crushed. "But I have to. You don't understand, this means everything to me."

"Does it?" Anderson snarled. "When was the last time you went to class? Maybe you need to start coming to terms with what's more important to you. Do you want to play games, or do you want to carry out secret missions and defend America?"

"I want to defend America. And make my dad proud," Mia said confidently.

Anderson looked skeptical.

"Do you think your dad would be proud if he saw your dorm room?" Before Mia could respond, Anderson darted over to the doorway and peered inside. "Look at it! It's covered in trash! Jack Daniel's bottles everywhere. Condom packets sprinkled on the floor. You ought to be ashamed of yourself, young lady."

"I promise . . . I'm going to change . . ." Tears began to form in her eyes. "Starting tomorrow, no more booze. No more boys. I'm focusing on my studies."

Just then Mia's roommate, Alice Lee, came up behind them. "What's going on?" she asked.

"Good evening, Private Cobra," Anderson said.

"Is Sparrow in trouble again?" said Alice.

"Get in your dorm room, Private. This doesn't concern you."

Alice giggled. "Oooo, it was a boy, wasn't it?"

"What makes you say that?" Mia asked.

"You aren't wearing a top underneath your hoodie." Alice turned to Anderson. "Was she caught red-handed again?"

"Go to your dorm room, Private Cobra, or I'm giving you twenty demerits."

"Busted," Alice snickered, then complied with Anderson's demand. Captain Anderson promptly slammed the door in Alice's face.

Seething, she narrowed her eyes on Mia. "Sparrow, I'm sorry, but I think I need to report this. I'm afraid you're going to have to be expelled this time."

"Wait! Wait!" She panicked. Mia tried to think of a way to persuade Captain Anderson, but ideas just weren't coming. "I'm going to turn over a new leaf. I promise."

"Tell you what, Private Sparrow. If you can make it until the end of the semester without getting a single demerit, I won't tell the Dean."

Mia's eyes sparkled with hope. "You don't have to worry, Captain. I'm going to get straight A's."

"I'll believe that when I see it."

Chapter 2

"MIA?" Alice asked, running to her side. "Is that you? I barely recognized you. Why are you like, dressed as a man?"

"It's called a suit, you dork-a-saurus. Successful people wear them."

"It's not *you*. Where's the usual crop top?"

"Only little girls wear crop tops. I'm an adult now. A secret agent in the making," Mia said.

Alice laughed. "I hardly think you count as an adult. Are you going to *class*?"

"Don't sound so surprised," Mia said.

"So . . . who was the guy?"

"What guy?" Mia asked.

"The one from last night, duh."

Mia rolled her eyes. "Someone I met."

"And *how* did you guys meet?" Alice prodded.

Mia rolled her eyes. "You don't wanna know."

"What does that mean?"

"Nothing."

"Was there any cash exchanged?" Alice questioned, tying her jet-black hair into a ponytail.

Mia punched her in the shoulder. "You're such a bitch-face! Don't be jealous. Besides, he drives an Audi and he knows a lot about politics. I think he's rich, too."

"Sounds like you have a real catch there, Sparrow."

They walked in silence for a moment.

"Are you like, getting expelled?" Alice asked.

"Of course not. You know who my dad is. Anderson let me go, like always, free and clear." Mia was pretty sure that Alice didn't hear the ultimatum Anderson had given her in the hallway the night before, so she thought it best that Alice not know the direness of the situation.

"I bet she did." Alice snickered. "You always talk about your dad. How come you never talk about your mom, Mia?"

Mia didn't want to discuss her mother. She changed the subject suddenly. "I have to go to Stealth Tactics." She turned at a right angle and headed away.

Alice followed her. "First bell is in ten whole minutes. Come get coffee with me." She grabbed Mia's hand and pulled her along.

"No, really, I have to go," Mia insisted.

"C'mon, I wanna hear more about this mystery guy."

"He's not a mystery."

"He has tattoos. I saw his police sketch."

"So?"

"Hello? Earth to Mia: do the math. If he's got money and has tattoos, that can only mean he's involved in organized crime."

The two of them worked evening shifts at a coffee shop at Pacific Beach called Sugar Dreams Coffee.

Once inside the coffee shop, they walked up to the counter. Mia ordered an espresso but pronounced it "expresso." Alice ordered the same but pronounced it correctly.

They took seats by a window and Mia gazed outside to the ocean view of Pacific Beach.

"We met on a pursuit," Mia started.

"You mean like, on assignment?"

"Yeah."

"It was at Six Flags."

Alice's mouth dropped. "No way. Wait, wait—was this at the Six Flags robbery last week?"

"Yeah."

"Oh my God, that's crazy! Was he one of the hostages?"

"Nope," Mia replied smugly.

Pause.

"He was the gunman," Mia blurted.

"You mean, that guy on TV?"

"His name is Jason."

"Shut up. I don't believe you."

"Why would I lie to you about this, Alice?"

"You're dating a *target*?" Alice convulsed in laughter.

"Keep your voice down," Mia whispered, eyes darting around nervously. "Besides, we're not 'dating.' We're just seeing each other."

"Oh my God oh my God! This is like, insane. Tell me how it happened."

Mia sighed. "Okay, so I was with my lead."

"Which one?"

"Agent Dolphin."

"No way!"

"And she got assigned to a pursuit," Mia explained. "Some crazed gunman apparently broke into Six Flags the night before and rewired the circuitry to one of the roller coasters."

"Right, right, I heard about it on the news. How come you never told me?"

"You didn't need to know." She cleared her throat and continued: "So then, we go down there, and I see the gunman has a microphone and some sort of remote control in his hand. So the roller coaster is stuck upside down with people trapped inside. So you heard how the gunman planted a bomb in it and was demanding ransom money?"

"Yeah."

"Well, I wanted to lead, but Dolphin told me I wasn't ready and that freshmen aren't allowed to lead on a pursuit under any circumstances."

"And let me guess . . . You disobeyed her," Alice said.

"Well, it wasn't really my fault, because Jason started it."

"What did he do?"

"Dolphin and I approached him, but he immediately locked eyes with me like I was the most beautiful thing he'd seen in all his life."

"I'm sure he did," Alice challenged.

"Anyways, he asked me what my name was, completely oblivious to Dolphin."

"And what did you tell him?" Alice asked.

"I told him I was Agent Sparrow. Of the Black Penguins."

"And?"

"And we exchanged phone numbers and started talking."

"In the middle of a hostage situation?"

"He's pretty hot, don't you think?" Mia said.

"Kinda hard to tell based on the police sketch."

"Yeah. So then, Dolphin butted in. Wanting to lead the pursuit. She tried to negotiate with him on the hostages."

"And then what happened?"

"I don't know. I mean, the last thing I remember was a puff of smoke. Then I woke up at headquarters in sick bay."

"He was holding hostages for ransom with a bomb and then he asked you out on a date?"

"Actually I asked him out."

"What?" Alice asked.

"I texted him."

"What did you say? 'Thanks for knocking me unconscious while I was supposed to be training to lead a pursuit?'"

"No, I was like, what can I text him that would be funny? Make him laugh."

"And what did you come up with?"

"Here. Take a look." Mia showed her the text that kicked it all off.

I'm available for ransom this weekend if ur not doing anything. ;)

"You're unbelievable," Alice said.

"You haven't seen his biceps."

"What are you gonna do?" Alice asked.

"Well, he likes kick-boxing, so I was thinking I'd sign up for a membership at his gym."

"Mia, you're crazy! You're only eighteen, and he's a deranged criminal. Probably even a serial killer. His name most likely isn't even Jason."

"No, no, Alice, you don't understand. He doesn't lie to me. His name is definitely Jason. Jason Smith."

"Okay, that is like, the most generic name in the universe," Alice said.

"Yeah, it's popular for a reason. It's a hot-sounding name."

"Have you seen his driver's license? How you jus' gonna believe everything he says so quickly?"

"He wouldn't lie to me. I can feel it," Mia said with a twinkle in her eye.

"You can't keep seeing him," Alice stated.

"Why not?"

"Mia, as soon Ingleton faculty find out that a student is dating a target, that's it. Kiss the Agency goodbye."

"But I'm a Black Penguin."

"Your dad's a Penguin. You're just a lowly Private, Mia."

"Don't worry," Mia assured her. "He started growing his beard out. In a couple of months, no one is even going to remember the whole Six Flags thing."

"People don't usually forget terrorist attacks so easily."

"He's not a terrorist. He's an entrepreneur."

"Has he killed anybody?" Alice asked.

"Don't be ridiculous." Mia had chosen to ignore this possibility during the past few days of seeing Jason.

"He's code seven, Mia. The Agency doesn't give permission to kill a target unless it's like, really serious."

Before Mia could retaliate, she suddenly grabbed Alice's hand and consulted her wristwatch.

8:59.

"Shit, now I'm going to be late! I didn't hear first bell. Did you hear it?"

"Since when do you care about getting to class on time?" Alice asked with a chuckle.

"I'm going to get demerits for this. Now I have to pray for some sort of miracle. I hate you, Alice!"

Without wasting another instant, Mia grabbed her backpack and bolted for the door. In the process, she tripped over her own foot and crash-landed into the arms of a guy in an Ingleton T-shirt who was waiting in line.

"I'm sorry!" she said.

Alice laughed. "I hate you too, Mia. Have a good day. See you at work tonight."

Chapter 3

BY the time Mia got to Stealth Tactics 10A, all of the other students had paired up and were preparing for the wall climb, fiddling with retractable cables and suction-cupped gloves.

"Sorry I'm late," Mia said to Agent Mongoose, the teacher of the class. Mongoose was a fit man in his forties who never bothered with small talk. He was simultaneously feared and hated by all the students.

"It's five past o' nine hundred, Private Sparrow." He scowled.

"I know, but you see, I had some 'issues' I had to deal with."

"That's your best excuse? Can't you at least come up with a creative lie?"

"No, you don't understand. I was dealing with some 'girl drama.' "

"Sparrow, you think an agent is allowed to have 'girl drama'? This isn't a damn day care center, this is Ingleton," shouted Mongoose.

"I'm sorry, but I was sort of having a 'heart-to-heart' with a friend of mine."

"I'm going to have to give you ten demerits for this, Private Sparrow."

Then, remembering her promise to Anderson, she sputtered out her next words pathetically. "Please please please, no!" She grabbed his arm and looked him dead in the eyes with a pleading look. "My dad is going to kill me."

"Not if I kill you first." He pulled his arm away.

"What if . . ." Her mind raced, concocting deals she could throw at him to negate the demerits. "What if I can climb the wall *red* in under two minutes?"

"None of the obstacles are to be attempted red for freshmen. Only green your freshman year."

(In agent terminology, "red" means to overcome an obstacle or apprehend a target without the assistance of specialized gear. "Green" means you have the best gear possible, and "blue" means you improvise with your environment.)

"Ten demerits says I can do it. I bet you even the upperclassmen can't do it in two minutes," Mia bragged.

"Sparrow, I'm not bending the rules for you. It's not going to work with me."

Mia upped the stakes. "I'll bet you ten demerits I can get up the wall red . . . faster than *you* can."

If Mia knew anything about guys, it was that their one weak spot was their pride.

"Don't be absurd. You're a freshman. I'm an agent."

"Sounds like someone's being a big chicken. *Chicken-Mongoose*," she teased. She made quacking sounds and flapped her arms.

Agent Mongoose dropped his clipboard onto the pavement and sneered. "That's a duck sound. Chickens don't *quack*."

Mia continued the taunt relentlessly.

Mongoose caved in finally. "Fine. You're on, Sparrow."

Agent Mongoose had never seen Mia climb before in Stealth class. Up until then they had been focusing on camouflage and navigating ventilation systems. He didn't know that Mia, despite her frail appearance, possessed a hidden talent.

Mia had absolutely no fear of heights whatsoever. In fact, she had been climbing things as long as she could remember. Her parents were rock climbers and so was she. Climbing was in her blood.

They used the six-story Artillery building as the training ground for this obstacle. It was made of brick and had overhanging ledges. Mia noted a slim rain gutter system, but nothing substantial to really hold onto.

Mia and Mongoose stood poised at the foot of the wall.

"On my count," Mongoose said. "One . . . Two . . . *Three!*"

Mia got to a promising start, taking the lead early. Being lightweight and nimble, she maneuvered her way up the wall deftly, leaving Mongoose in the dust. She nearly reached the top, passing other students who were climbing the wall green with ropes and safety equipment, when one of them called out to her.

"Hey, Sparrow, you sure are climbing up that wall fast! What's up there, a Costco-sized box of condoms?" he taunted.

This broke Mia's concentration. The implications of the insult pissed her off so much that she nearly slipped and fell to her death.

It was a boy. He looked gangly and surfer-like. Mangy long hair and unnaturally lean features. Definitely not her type.

"Just who the hell do you think you are?" she asked.

"Pablo. Pablo Honey," he said calmly.

"Like the Radiohead album?"

"Actually it's just a coincidence."

"What kind of a stupid name is *that*?" she countered. "Sounds like a porn star name to me."

"I wouldn't know. I don't have too many porn star friends." He smirked.

Now she was really flustered. "Sorry, I'm confused. Do we know each other?"

"We do now."

"Do you know who I am?"

"Sure, you're Mia Rojas. You're a descendant of Black Penguins."

"And how do you know that?" Mia asked.

"I have Interrogation 20B with your roommate."

"Alice?"

"She talks about you all the time," Pablo said.

"What does she say?" Mia began to worry about the musings between her roommate and this obnoxious surfer.

"Just like, funny stories about the two of you. I figured you could take a joke or two."

"Is this your way of an introduction?"

"You catch on quick."

"What's your codename?" Mia asked.

"Wombat. And yours is Sparrow."

Meanwhile, Mongoose had reached the top of the wall and announced his victory. "Twenty demerits, missy!"

"No!" She turned to Pablo. "Dammit, Pablo, look what you made me do!" Her hands shook and she could feel her heart thumping fiercely in her throat. Would Mongoose actually give her the demerits? Would Anderson find out about them? No, of course not. She presumed that, should push ever come to shove, her dad would give the school his two cents and they'd wipe the slate clean for her.

"Hey, if you can't keep your cool during a training simulation, what makes you think you can keep it together in a real-life crisis?" Pablo said.

"You asshole! Now I'm in trouble because of you!"

He smiled.

"I hate you!" Mia shouted.

"Do you want to use my rope?" he offered.

"No. I don't need your help."

"How are you going to get down?" Pablo asked.

"I'm not going down."

"That's hard to believe, considering what I've heard." Pablo sneered.

"Shut up, *Porn Star Pablo*. I'm going to finish the obstacle. I'm going *up*," she said with the most dignity she could muster.

"Suit yourself, Sparrow."

Mia continued climbing. She tried to focus her mind on the placement of her hands and feet and not on Pablo's snide remarks.

"Do you surf?" he asked, struggling to keep pace with her.

"Why do you ask?" she replied. She didn't bother with any form of eye contact.

"You just look like you surf," he said.

"This *is* San Diego. Would it be a stretch if I said yes?"

"Probably not," said Pablo.

"Okay, then yeah, I surf." In truth Mia didn't even know how to stand on a board, much less ride a wave. But she wanted to dispel any notions that she was an immature party girl, so she exaggerated a little. "I go every morning before school, in fact."

"So do I," he said. "Where do you go surfing at?"

"Sunset Cliffs."

"I've never seen you there," Pablo said.

"I go early, well before sunrise . . ."

"You surf in the dark? How do you see the breaks?" Pablo asked.

"When you've been surfing as long as I have, you can feel the waves . . . Are you going to ask me out on a surf date or something?"

"Not yet," he replied.

"Well, what are you waiting for?"

"The waves are too big right now."

"You scared of big waves?" Mia asked in a mocking tone.

"No, they're too big for you. For me they're perfect."

"Okay, if not a surf date, what kind of date are you going to ask me out *on*?"

"I never said I'd ask you out on a date. Sounds like you're asking me to ask you out."

"I have a boyfriend," she replied smugly.

"Not what I heard. Heard it wasn't anything serious."

How did he know? Had Alice gossiped that quick? Maybe he was bluffing.

"It is," Mia insisted. "Very serious. And I wouldn't expect *you* to understand these type of things. It's . . . it's a committed relationship."

He chuckled. "You think he'd call it a 'relationship' too?"

"Of course, he's my boyfriend," she repeated, clinging precariously to the rain gutter.

"Boyfriend. Funny, I've never heard the words 'boyfriend' and 'Mia' mixed in the same sentence before."

"Well, get used to it. Because starting today, *I* am a new leaf."

She reached the top and sighed in utter relief to be off the wall safely.

"I see. So this new leaf gets twice as many demerits as the old leaf?" He snickered.

"Shut up."

"What do you have second period?" he asked, finally reaching the top of the wall himself.

"None of your business." She crossed her arms but didn't look away from his charming hazel eyes either.

"I have Cryptography 20A."

"You do not."

"Not unless my schedule is messed up and I've been going to the wrong class for months."

"That can't be right. I have Cryptography too," Mia said.

"What a coincidence. Almost as if it was meant to be."

"Why haven't I ever seen you in class before?" she asked.

"You would have to actually *go* to class to see me. And *you* never show up."

"Well, I'm going to all my classes now," she replied.

"Good. Looks like we'll be seeing a lot of each other then."

This was an utter nightmare. Two classes with this boy? One was bad enough.

Chapter 4

"I need to unwind," Mia mumbled, working on a drawing of a mouse with a machine gun shooting bullet after bullet into a cartoon rendition of Agent Mongoose.

Sugar Dreams Coffee was filled with students, most of them quietly studying for their midterms that week.

"I heard you met a boy today," Alice said. Mia glanced up at her.

"You mean that twerp Pablo?" Mia went back to her drawing.

"I think he has a crush on you," Alice said.

"Ew. And what the hell are you doing gossiping about me in class for, anyway?"

"I'm not gossiping. Just chatting it up with people. Making friends."

"He's so lewd," Mia said. "I wouldn't want to be friends with someone like that."

Mia's lips pursed into a slight reflexive grin that lasted only a nanosecond or so, but Alice saw it. "Oh my God!" she said, reacting as if Mia's face had just melted off.

"What?" Mia asked, suddenly concerned for her safety.

"You *like* him!"

"I do not!"

"Yes you do. I can so see it in your eyes."

Mia blushed. She tried to compose herself, but she knew Alice could see her cheeks redden.

Pablo's chiseled features were striking, but he was too skinny. His eyes were bright and delightful, but behind them was an insidious glare.

"I have a boyfriend, for one thing. And he's not my type. Not at all," Mia insisted. The guy's crassness was just way over the top and it put Mia in a queasy state of unease.

"Okay, first off, you do *not* have a boyfriend. And second, if Jason hasn't been arrested yet, he's probably plotting to murder you in your sleep at this very moment."

A text popped onto Mia's phone just then, which was lying face-up on the countertop. "Speak of the devil, is that him?" Alice asked. "Let me see."

Alice snatched the phone, but Mia wrestled with her to get it back. "Give it, you cunt-face!" Mia yelled, but it was useless. Alice had clear possession.

"Let me read it," Alice snapped, her arm twisted behind her back. Mia shoved her up against the bean tubs. One of them fell over onto the ground, spilling coffee beans all over the floor.

"You're cleaning that up," Mia said.

"Nah-ah. We agreed. You do mopping and I do register count."

The struggle continued. "You always—get to do—register count! I'm doing it from now on," Mia argued.

"Are you a roaster? Are you certified? *No.* Respect seniority, Mia."

"Dammit, Alice, I hate you!" Unable to retrieve her phone from Alice, Mia grabbed a nearby spatula and waved it like a katana in front of her face.

"Whatchu gonna do with that, bitch?" Alice threatened, then turned her attention to the phone and read Jason's text message aloud.

" 'Netflix?' "

Her eyes rose to Mia. "It's a booty call!"

"Give me my phone back!"

The spectacle was drawing attention from customers and a few had begun snickering discreetly. Some looked worried, others downright amused.

"Give me your thumb, Mia. I'm replying to him." She grabbed Mia's wrist, then forcibly pressed Mia's finger against the phone's "unlock" button.

"Stop!"

Mia swatted her with the spatula repeatedly, but it did very little to deter Alice from typing out a response to Jason.

"You hoe-bag! Stop! Stop!" Mia yelled, now sweating and frantic.

Mercifully, a customer saved Mia in the nick of time before Alice could hit "send."

"Can I order a drink?" the customer asked sternly.

The two girls untangled themselves from each other and took places back at the register with fake smiles painted on their faces, panting like wild dogs.

Alice cleared her throat and spoke up. "Welcome to Sugar Dreams." She shot Mia a derisive glance. "What can I get for you?"

"Can I get a . . . double raspberry latte?" he asked.

Alice manned the register, pressing a few buttons.

Mia, meanwhile, smiled and winked at the customer. "Watch this," she said confidently, then grabbed a nearby Torani syrup bottle and flipped it up behind her back, hoping to catch it impressively in mid-air. It twirled up, but she forgot to screw the cap on, and syrup sprayed all over the place, dousing the poor customer with sticky red liquid.

Mia missed the bottle on its way down and it fell to the ground with a crash. She shrieked in horror and took a step back.

"What the fuck! What kind of coffee shop is this?" the customer said with red raspberry syrup dripping down his chin and eyebrows. "I'm going to Starbucks." He grabbed a napkin and wiped his face as best he could, then headed straight for the door. Before leaving, he stopped in his tracks, turned his head over his shoulder, and added: "I'm writing a Yelp review."

Mia's eyes widened. "No!" She ran after him. "Please, don't. My boss reads them."

He narrowed his eyes at her. "This place used to be the best. Now it's nothing but a bunch of dumb college kids rough-housing like preschoolers."

At that, he stormed off out the door.

Mia, now distraught, turned to face Alice, who hadn't budged from her post at the register. "What am I going to do?" Mia asked.

Alice grinned. "You take things too seriously, Mia. You need to loosen up. It's not that big a deal."

A guy with glasses and a sweater wrapped around his waist rose from his chair, abandoned his textbook, and strode up to the counter. "Would you two knock it off? I can't get any studying done with all this racket."

Without so much as a blink, Alice opened a nearby drawer, shuffled through it, and pulled out a pair of earbuds. She bundled them up and tossed them over to the glasses guy.

"Listen to some dubstep," she suggested.

He grimaced, then threw the headphones on the floor in disgust. He gathered up his things, crammed them haphazardly into his backpack, and stormed out the door in protest, giving them the finger on his way out.

"Alice, you crazy shit, we're going to get in trouble," Mia said.

"You, Sparrow, need a drink." Alice smiled. "We're closing up early."

Alice climbed up onto the granite countertop. Heads turned in her direction. She cleared her throat. "Okay, so . . . um, the coffee shop is like, closing up early tonight . . . so . . . like . . . you need to go."

She held up a hand, fingers extended. "Five minutes."

Mia was appalled. No one said a word for a few awkward moments.

Then Alice broke the silence. "Thanks." She hopped off the countertop.

Slowly the customers gathered up their things and headed out. All but one, however.

"The sign says ten o'clock," said a girl with braided red hair and a look of contempt on her face. "Some of us have midterms to study for."

"I'm the manager. We have a company-wide meeting at the Bubble Factory," Alice said, referring to the bar next door to the coffee shop (which got its name from a machine inside that blew a stream of bubbles throughout the bar).

"You're not the manager," the girl challenged. "And you're not twenty-one either. I've seen you in class. Your name is Alice Lee. *Freshman*."

"Well, in class, I'm just a student, but here, I'm Alice Lee, CEO of Sugar Dreams. And I decide what time I open and close my business. I have all the power."

"You do not. Tony owns this place," the girl said. "And when he finds out you guys are kicking customers out the door, he won't be too happy."

Alice contorted her lips into a scowl, then grabbed the keys off the girl's table and promptly tossed them across the room to Mia. "Catch!"

The keys sailed through Mia's hands and hit her in the forehead. "Ow! What the hell kind of a throw was that? Jesus, Alice!"

"Quick!" Alice said. "Go find her car in the parking lot and drive it into a telephone pole!"

"What the hell!" said the girl. "Have you guys lost your minds? Give me back my keys!" She chased after Mia, who ducked out the back without forethought, slamming the kitchen door behind her and locking it. Alice, meanwhile, was probably rupturing her spleen from laughing too hard.

The girl darted down the room to the front door and Alice followed suit. Mia had taken the shortcut to the parking lot and was frantically clicking the horn button trying to find which car was the girl's.

Then: a honk from a Toyota sedan.

Success!

The girl shouted from the far side of the parking lot, "Stop!"

She charged at Mia like a rabid bull.

Mia threw the keys over the girl's head and Alice caught them.

Alice turned to the beach and threw the keys heedlessly toward the volleyball nets into the poorly lit sand.

"We close at eight today," Alice said smugly. "Go get your keys."

"You asshole!" the girl yelled in response. She whipped out her phone and, using her screen as a flashlight, ran toward the direction of the keys' flight path, mumbling curse words to herself.

Alice wasted no time. "C'mon, Mia, let's go get a drink."

They ran back inside and Mia slammed the door shut.

"What if she calls the police?" Mia asked, with a shortness of breath and her heart racing.

Alice winked. "Then we play hard to get."

Chapter 5

FAKE IDs and six spent shot glasses lined the bar countertop.

"I wanna like, get some tacos," Alice said.

"With lots of sour cream," Mia added. Then amended her response: "No, I shouldn't. I need to slim down."

"Hello? Didn't you pay attention in Biology? Calories don't count if you don't remember them. Let's do another shot."

They each grabbed a glass of vodka, clinked each other, and Alice toasted: "To blackouts!"

"Blackouts," Mia parroted.

They swigged the shots down in unison while bubbles floated in the air around them.

Mia's eyes grew wide suddenly when she saw who was sitting at a table down by the other end of the bar. "Shit, it's him!"

"Who?" Alice asked.

"Your buddy Pablo—don't turn!"

Alice slid off the barstool and meandered over to the table where Pablo was sitting. A girl was sitting opposite him with carrot-colored hair. "C'mon, Mia, don't be shy."

"I'm not shy." She followed reluctantly.

Alice skipped the introductions entirely. She took a seat next to Pablo, crossed a leg over his, and wrapped her arm around his neck. Next she let her head collapse onto his shoulder and she grabbed his thigh with her other hand.

"Alice, is that you?" he asked.

"Why wouldn't it be me? Do girls just randomly come sit next to you in bars and start cuddling you without a word?"

"Well—"

She shook her head drunkenly so that her black hair pelted him in the face. "I've been using a new shampoo. Do you like it, Pablo Honey?" She shook her head a second time and Alice couldn't bring herself to stop giggling.

The hair onslaught continued. "What the hell, Alice!" Pablo asked, backing up against the wall.

Alice stopped, then looked Pablo directly in the eye. "Trying to make Mia jealous."

"Jealous of *what*?" Mia asked.

Alice got right up in Pablo's ear. "My friend Mia has a crush on a boy, and his name rhymes 'money.' "

"I do not!" Mia protested.

Pablo's buddy smiled at her and said, "You're Mia Rojas? Your dad is a Black Penguin, isn't he?"

"Yeah . . . So's my sister."

"Angel? That her?" she asked.

"Yeah, you know her?" Mia replied.

"She works in Domestic Ops."

"That's classified. How did you know that?"

"We have the same target. Sit down, have a beer." She scooted aside as if to make room for her.

"How do you and Pablo know each other?" Mia asked, taking a seat next to her.

"I just moved here from Ireland," she said. "Pablo's been teaching me to surf."

Alice interrupted them. "You should text her to come over here."

"Who?"

"Angel!"

"Here? To a bar at Pacific Beach to hang out with her drunken little sister and a strange guy?"

"Yeah!"

Mia was not exactly on good terms with her big sister. Secretly, she despised her for being so damn successful. Why did she always have to set the bar so high? Being the first born is the easiest. You can get away with murder if that's what you're into.

"Um, well, I'd assume she's at home watching Netflix on the couch with her *husband*." She said this last word the way a pastor says "demon" at a church sermon.

"Oh."

"Yeah, she doesn't do anything exciting." In her head Mia pictured images of her sister doing mundane chores. Sighing loudly during sex while checking her Facebook feed in boredom, then faking an orgasm. Anything to make her think that she had it better than her sister. "She's *married*."

"Sorry to hear that," said Pablo's friend. "By the way, I'm Bonnie." She had a delightfully innocent grin.

Pablo interjected. "Let's play a game."

"A game?" Alice said.

"What's it called? Choose a porn star name?" Mia asked, thinking herself witty. "Because you're clearly winning."

"You used that one already, for the record," Pablo said. "It's called 'truth or dare.'"

"What are we, in second grade?" Mia asked.

"No, no, it's gonna be fun. We take turns. You can either tell the truth, or you can do a dare."

"That sounds dumb," Mia said.

"Mia's starting us off," Alice proposed.

"I'm not playing."

"You have to," Pablo insisted.

"This game is stupid!" Mia said, folding her arms defiantly.

"Dare," Alice said with a sly look on her face.

"That's not how the game works. I get to choose. I want truth."

"I'm changing the rules. Mia can't do truth," Alice said.

"Why the hell not?" Mia asked.

"Um, because you like, always exaggerate stuff, duh," Alice said.

"I've got one for her. See that girl over there?" Pablo pointed.

"Which one?"

"The one with the red sweater."

"Yeah."

"I want you to get her number without saying a single word to her."

"That's stupid. Besides, I'm not a lesbian," Mia protested.

"That's not how the game works. She looks lonely, sitting by herself. C'mon, go show us a little seduction, Sparrow."

Mia rolled her eyes. "Shit . . ." After thinking a minute, an idea popped into Mia's head and she called for the bartender.

"What's your plan, Mia?" Alice asked.

"Shut up." She turned to the bartender. "Can I order ten carne asada tacos and a to-go box?"

"Sure," he replied.

"But they're not for me. Can you give them to the girl in the red sweater over there, and tell her they're from me?"

He looked at her oddly, but agreed.

"Tacos? Really?" Alice said.

"Watch this," Mia replied.

She focused closely on the girl like a puma hunting prey until the tacos landed on her table. The girl looked confused at first, then she locked eyes with Mia as soon as the bartender gestured in Mia's direction.

Chestnut hair, delicate features, and fair skin. Mia got up, walked over to her, and sat down in the booth beside her.

Their eyes interlocked. Mia smiled.

"What are you doing?" the girl asked warily.

Mia didn't break eye contact. She kept smiling. Scooted a little closer.

"Um, thanks for the tacos?" she said, more like a question than a statement.

Mia nodded.

"Why so many? I can't eat them all."

Mia pointed to herself, then to the girl, then shot her eyes briefly to the to-go box before bringing them back up to the girl's.

The girl smirked. "Have we met before?"

Mia pulled out her phone, unlocked it, and handed it to the girl. She raised her eyebrows and fluttered her eyelashes.

She giggled in confused amusement. "God, you're so weird! Do you always do this?"

Mia shrugged.

"Can you talk?" the girl asked.

Mia nodded.

The girl seemed at ease. "I'm Lisa. Codename Tiger. You go to Ingleton?"

Mia nodded, then pointed to the phone.

"You want my number?" the girl called Lisa said.

Mia smiled widely in response.

"God, you're like the weirdest person I've ever met . . . I've had a rough day today."

Without hesitation, Mia wrapped her arms around Lisa and hugged her.

"What are you doing?" said Lisa.

Mia held her as tight as she could.

At first Lisa struggled to free herself, but after a few seconds, she hugged Mia back.

Much to Mia's surprise, she heard her crying out of the blue, and Mia released her.

They held eye contact.

"You're like, the sweetest person I've ever met," said Lisa. "Honestly, you have no idea what I've gone through today." She wiped a few glistening tears from her eyes. "My boyfriend and I broke up this morning, and, and . . ."

Suddenly Mia had gone from absolute stranger to therapist in a matter of minutes.

"I just needed someone to listen." She wiped her eyes but wetness continued to roll out of them.

Mia grabbed a taco, took a bite, and bowed her head momentarily, as if to say, "no problem."

Lisa called for the bartender. "Let's take a shot together," she said.

Mia winked.

Lisa giggled. "A couple shots."

Chapter 6

MIA woke up to an unwelcome noise: Taylor Swift's "Blank Space." Normally it was her favorite song but now it just sounded like power tools sawing through blocks of concrete.

"Alice . . . Turn it off," Mia mumbled. She was lying on the floor upside down with her feet propped up on the bed.

"Ha ha, look at you! Do you even remember what happened last night?" Alice said while brushing her hair.

"Ughh!' Mia groaned, pulling a stray shoe off her stomach and climbing weakly onto her knees. Her head felt like an invisible woodpecker was hammering away repeatedly at it from various angles.

She freaked out when she saw the time: *8:55.*

"Why didn't you wake me up, Alice? I'm going to be late for class again!"

"Why didn't your alarm wake you up?" Alice responded.

Mia thought about it. "I don't know." She became frazzled just then. "Where's my phone?"

"Probably with your date."

"What date?"

"You don't remember, like, making out with that girl in the red sweater last night?"

"Shut up. What girl?"

"Oh my God, you don't even remember it?"

"Stop playing games, bitch. That didn't happen."

A hazy recollection swirled through her already racked brain; an image of the girl came vaguely to mind.

Chestnut hair.

Pale, fair skin.

Those big brown eyes. Staring into them.

"Lisa," Mia stated.

"Is that her name?"

"How did I get home?" Mia asked.

"I don't know. It wasn't with me, though. You left with that girl."

"I did not!"

8:57.

Without wasting another second, Mia rushed to find a matching shoe, uncovering books, papers, and dirty laundry.

"Where's my other shoe?"

"Maybe you left it at her house."

Horror spread across Mia's face. "Oh my God, Alice! She has my phone!"

"Do you know her last name? Or like, her codename?"

Mia struggled to recall the memory. "Rabbit? Gopher?"

It was no use. The memory was gone.

"I am like, freaking out right now! Why is this happening to me?"

"Relax, just get another one."

"A stranger has my phone, Alice! What if she's hacked into my Instagram account and is posting pictures of penises online?"

"Why would she do that, Mia?"

"I need to go to class. I—I can't believe this."

Stressed, shaking, and practically to the point of tears, Mia threw on a horrifically unfashionable ensemble of sweatpants, a beige hoodie, and sunglasses.

"Wait, Mia!" Alice called after her.

Mia didn't even bother replying. She ran down the hallway without sparing a second.

Alice followed close behind. "You can't go to class looking like that! Look at your hair, I think I see globs of guacamole stuck in it!"

Mia came to an abrupt stop.

Running a few fingers through her hair, she confirmed Alice's theory, which mortified her, and she screamed. "Oh my God, what the hell!"

"Ha ha, Mia, she has access to your texts! What if she steals your man?"

This realization brought Mia's heartbeat up to a sudden crescendo. "She can read his texts . . . What if she's replying to him? Pretending to me . . . Dammit, she's going to ruin everything!"

Mia snuck quietly into Stealth Tactics and took a seat in the back row, avoiding detection. She sighed deeply, now dealing with serious separation anxiety issues stemming from the loss of her phone.

Mongoose had his back turned; he was writing out methods of lockpicking on the chalkboard.

"What we have here is a standard bump key. This will open a standard lock."

While he drew a picture of a key on the board, a boy came over and took a seat beside Mia.

It was Pablo.

"What are you doing? You can't sit here," Mia whispered.

"Didn't think I'd be seeing *you* in class, not after last night."

"Why not? I was totally fine."

He smirked and shook his head. "I wouldn't consider throwing tacos at cheerleaders to be *fine*."

"What on earth are you talking about?" Mia asked.

"You don't remember? You and that girl in the red sweater?"

"You're making stuff up. We ate the tacos. We didn't throw them at anyone."

He laughed coarsely. "You mean you don't remember the taco fight?"

"What taco fight?"

"The Ingleton cheer squad. When they got to the bar? I'd be surprised if they let you set foot in the Bubble Factory again, after that *scene* you made."

"Shut up. That didn't happen."

"Go ask Alice. She was there," Pablo said.

"Why would I throw my tacos at the cheerleaders? That doesn't make any sense."

"You tell me. Who knows what's going on inside that batshit crazy head of yours. If you ask me, I think you're jealous."

Mia crossed her arms and legs on cue. "Jealous? Please . . . Of what?"

"Girls who are prettier than you."

She slapped him hard on the arm.

"You are such an asshole!" She turned her entire body in the opposite direction.

"Relax, Mia. You know it's all surgery."

"Is that supposed to be a compliment?"

"I don't think you even really *need* surgery. Maybe just a little ego-suction."

"I am *not* having this conversation right now." Without her phone, though, she had nothing to pretend to look busy, so she started taking notes.

"What happened to your hair?" he teased.

"Go away." No eye contact.

"I have some shampoo you can borrow. For the insects, though, you might wanna try Raid."

Silent treatment.

"Just worried about your safety. I just don't want you getting shot."

"Why the *hell* would I get shot?" she asked angrily, finally facing him.

"You might get mistaken for bigfoot."

"That's *it*. I'm getting out of here!"

Agent Mongoose spoke up from the front of the classroom. "Private Sparrow! Is there a problem?"

All eyes were on her.

"No . . . Sorry." She went meekly back to her seat. She definitely wanted to avoid attention, especially with her disheveled appearance.

"If I hear so much as a peep out of you for the rest of class, I'm giving you ten demerits," Mongoose threatened.

Mia spent the remainder of the class drawing pictures of barnyard animals with weapons, trying her best to ignore Pablo, who was tapping his pencil against his desk in a highly un-rhythmic and annoying manner.

"Remember, midterms tomorrow."

The bell rang and Mia pounced out of her seat and went straight for the door, making a noticeable effort to bump Pablo on her way out.

Chapter 7

AS soon as Mia got out the classroom door, she felt a hand grab her arm. She spun around.

It was a brunette with smiley eyes and a blushing face.

"Mia?" she said. "Hi . . . It's me. Lisa."

Lisa, Lisa, Lisa.

She thought through the Lisas she knew. None of them looked like this one.

"From the Bubble Factory," she said.

Lisa! This was her! The girl from last night!

"Oh! How did you know I was going to be here?"

"Your phone. You left it in my car."

She handed Mia the phone and her heart leapt for joy.

"Oh thank you so much! I was so worried about it."

"No problem."

"But how did you find me?" Mia asked.

"Well, you left it unlocked, and you don't have a timer on it . . ."

"Oh . . ."

"So I posted on Facebook."

"Facebook? You mean *my* Facebook?"

"Yeah, I just asked if anyone knows what classes you have, so I could find you. Someone named Kathy said you have Stealth first period . . . I didn't do any snooping . . ."

"Oh, uh, it's okay . . ." She doubted very much the girl didn't do a little rummaging through the phone. Immediately she scrolled through texts, but found none from Jason.

A missed call. Her eyes widened.

Shit.

It was from her dad.

"Can you give me one sec? I just need to call someone back."

"Sure, no problem, Mia." The girl was extra smiley but it didn't stop her from worrying about the call from her dad.

Then she heard that cold, dark voice of her father.

"Hello."

"Dad. It's me. Hi. How are you?" she asked with feigned warmth in her tone.

"Cut the shit, Mia. I got a call from the school. What's this I hear about you facing expulsion?"

"What?"

"Mia, you listen to me, and you listen good. You go apologize to whoever you need to apologize to. You do whatever it takes. You get down on your hands and knees and beg if you have to. Don't disappoint me, Mia. I'm warning you—"

"Wait, Dad, let me explain!"

"Mia, if you get expelled from Ingleton, that's it. *Se acabo*. You are no longer my daughter. You'll have to get your last name changed. I'm disowning you."

"Dad, come on, you're not serious—"

"Permanently," he added coldly.

"Dad! This is *so* unfair! I've been framed!"

"I doubt that."

"Wait! Wait!"

"Don't even think about calling back unless you have settled this business with the school. And I am *not* helping you out either."

"Would you listen to—"

"Bye, Mia."

Click.

Shit.

"Is everything okay?" Lisa asked.

"Why does this kind of thing only happen to me?" Tears began welling up in her eyes.

Lisa put her arms around Mia and hugged her. "It's okay. Look, one day, when we're both secret agents, we'll look back on this and laugh."

Mia wasn't as optimistic. Lisa pulled back and smiled at her.

"*Agent* Sparrow," she said.

"I'm never going to be an agent now," Mia said in a shaky voice.

"Not with that attitude. Look, just focus on positive thoughts. So, tell me why you're here at Ingleton. Why do you want to be an agent?"

"My parents," Mia said. "I want to make them proud."

"Your dad's a Black Penguin. What about your mom? Is she an agent too?"

"Well . . ." Mia began. "They met as Privates at Ingleton. My dad graduated first and made Penguin only a year later."

"Yeah, he was the one who killed that crime lord 'Machete Jack.' I read about him in Target History 20A. Your dad's a legend."

"Yeah, but my mom never graduated. She just dropped out as soon as my dad got transcripted," Mia explained.

"Well, sure. If you had a Black Penguin husband, you'd never have to work a day in your life again."

"Yeah, but . . . I just always kind of . . ."

"Kind of what?"

Mia bit her lip. She didn't want to talk about her mother and how she secretly felt sorry for her. The mother who took the easy way out.

Mia admired her father because he was revered. Her biggest fear was that she'd end up like her mother: no real accomplishments of her own. She never told this to anyone. Not her father, not her sister, not even Alice. No one.

She was only eighteen, but her fear was a ticking time bomb, a lake of magma boiling beneath her. The fear that one day, she would turn into her mother. One day, she'd become "obsolete."

Permanently.

Like her mother.

"I need to talk to the Dean. Lisa, I'm in so much trouble."

Just then a text popped onto her screen.

Sup.

It was Jason.

"Jason!" she shouted in a voice of electric glee.

Perhaps he'd be able to threaten someone at the school to remove the motion to expel from her record.

She typed:

> *Can u punch someone for me?*

Send.

> *I'm in trouble I need you Jason!*

She waited. Nothing. Dammit, Jason, why do you always take so long to reply to text messages?

No response.

"Do you know where the Dean is?" Mia asked Lisa.

"Sure. Headquarters."

"Oh, he's not on campus? Do you know which floor he's on?"

"I mean, I've never met him. He's at the top, they say." Lisa chuckled. "But you can't just waltz into his office. You need to be admitted."

Mia ran her hands nervously through her hair. Upon finding a clump of God-knows-what in it, threw a hideous brown object onto the pavement and shrieked.

"What is *that*?" Lisa asked with a cocked eyebrow.

"I have no idea," Mia said.

Lisa inspected it with a flip-flop. "Looks like a piece of meat." She grinned. "Is that from the taco fight last night?"

Not wanting to discuss the events at the Bubble Factory, Mia changed the subject. "I need to see about talking with the Dean."

"Good luck getting in," Lisa replied. "Oh. I forgot to ask you. Are you missing a shoe?"

"Why?" Mia asked.

"I think you left one in my car last night. Don't worry, I have it in my room. What Hall are you in?"

"Pistachio Hall," Mia replied.

"No kidding? How'd you get admitted *there*?"

"I happen to be very smart," she said, though in truth it was her father who used his "influence" to get her in.

"I'm in Rosebud Hall," Lisa replied. "Maybe you can come get it after school?"

"I'd like to, but I have to study for mid-terms." Rosebud was where all the nerdy girls stayed.

A bell rang just then.

"I should be getting to class," Lisa said. She gave Mia a longing look. "We should hang out sometime."

"Of course," Mia said.

"I am looking for a roommate," Lisa said, "in case you ever want to join Rosebud."

"I'll keep it in mind," Mia said, but in actuality she'd have been mortified to do anything of the sort.

Mia turned and headed toward the black twenty-story Agency building looming on the horizon.

"You're going now?" Lisa asked.

"Sure. Why not?"

"Don't you have to go to class?"

"Well, if I'm expelled, then I won't even have a class to go *to*," Mia said.

Chapter 8

THE headquarters building was air-conditioned and devoid of any sort of décor. When she reached the end of a long stainless steel hall, she saw a big metal door and a group of four armed guards decked out in black suits. They looked like they hit the gym twice a day and were as stone-faced as gargoyles.

"Hi there, boys," Mia said, approaching the men with a slight sashay in the hips.

"State your business here," said one of them robotically.

"Just thought I'd come to see you, stud." She threw him a little wink and cocked her head back so that her hair blew about her shoulders.

"We have a dress code," another one said smugly, eyeing her up and down.

Mia felt rather appalled at the comment, but instead of letting it get to her, she turned the tables on him. "*My* suit's at the cleaners. Think I could borrow yours, handsome?" She caressed the sleeve of his jacket.

He chuckled. "Are you a student?"

"I'm a freshman. Agent Sparrow's the name."

"*Private* Sparrow," one of the guards corrected.

"What are you doing here? Why aren't you in class?"

"I don't need to go."

"Why not? Aren't midterms starting this week?"

"I don't have mine 'til tomorrow."

"Shouldn't you be studying then?"

"You don't need to study when you have natural talent."

He smirked. "What makes you think you're even going to pass? You haven't taken a single midterm since you got here, freshman."

"I have *Penguin* in my blood," Mia said triumphantly.

"Oh, I think I know who you are. Agent Ostrich? That your sister?"

"That's the one."

One of the guards turned to the guy next to him, and said, "Ostrich. Not my favorite."

"We don't get along," Mia said.

"What are you here for?"

"I need to speak with the Dean," she said.

"What do you want to talk to the Dean about?"

"I want to see about getting into some AP classes. My course load is just too easy for me."

"Make an appointment with your counselor like every other student. The Dean is going to laugh if I bring you up there uninvited. And the sweatpants aren't helping, either."

"I'm sure we can find some way . . ." She added a few purposefully aimed eyelash flicks for good measure.

"Let me look you up." He scrolled through menus on his phone. Then, his face morphed into a sudden smirk and he erupted in laughter.

"What's so funny?" she asked, confused.

He handed the phone to his fellow guard and he too began to laugh.

"Did anyone tell you that you got *expelled* this morning?" he said.

"What? You must have the wrong person." She had hoped she wouldn't have to tell the truth to them, but she pretended like it was news to her.

"I'm afraid we can't let you in this building, not unless you're escorted by a student or a faculty member."

"No! Please, I have to speak with the Dean!"

He snickered. "C'mon, miss. Let's get you out of here. Jamison, you mind showing her the door?"

"Certainly." Jamison stepped forward and grabbed her by the arm.

"Stop! Let go of me! Do you know who my father is?"

The guard shoved her out the door and she stumbled clumsily down the stone steps of headquarters.

"You'll be sorry," Mia warned, but the guard merely shook his head at her in dismay.

"Have a good day."

He closed the door.

Why oh why? Her worst nightmare was coming true.

She tried to grasp hold of her thoughts. *Think, Mia. Devise a plan.*

She checked her phone. Jason was of no use, not even bothering with a response. So she texted him again:

Help! I'm being attacked by a dragon!

No response still.

Alice!

She typed out a message to her:

Alice, I need your help! I got expelled and I need u to come with me to talk to the dean!

Her heart raced. Her veins felt like they had been filled with high-octane gasoline. Sweat trickled down her brow.

Defeated, she took a seat at the foot of the stairs and buried her head in her hands.

She felt a nudge on her shoulder.

She looked up.

It was a guy in a suit holding a five dollar bill out to her.

"What?" she asked, confused.

"For a meal," he said. "I know of a homeless shelter in North Park. I can give you a ride."

"I'm not homeless!" she yelled, swatting the dollar away.

A message popped onto her phone from Alice:

No way! Haha.

    Alice, this is serious! I need your help!
Wait are you joking?

                    No!

Where are you?

By the headquarters building.

Get ur 'boyfriend' to come get you.

He hasn't responded yet.

You texted him?

Yah.

Ok I can come by at lunch.

Kk. I'll wait. And can you stop by the hall and bring a decent pair of jeans?

Haha you lagoon creature! lololol

It's not funny! ☹

Chapter 9

MIA'S heart soared when she saw Alice coming down the street, a fresh pair of jeans in hand.

Thank God.

"You look like you just got back from a week of Burning Man," Alice said, with a gleam of superiority in her tone.

"Shut up, at least I have real eyebrows," Mia said, mocking the thin lines tattooed on Alice's face.

Alice tossed Mia the jeans.

"There's nowhere to change," Mia said, looking around nervously for a bathroom.

"Just put them over your hobo pants."

Mia kicked off her shoes and slipped the jeans on over her sweatpants.

Alice grinned. "Now it just makes your legs look fat."

"Whatever, bitch, I see you checking me out when I do my calf raises. I know you're jealous as hell."

"But you can't even do ten of them in a row," Alice said.

"Please, I do over a hundred a day now. I do them in the shower."

"Sure you do . . ."

They opened the door to the long stainless steel hall and walked toward the guards.

"Do you have a plan?" Mia asked.

"I was thinking I'd sell your bed on Craigslist. The dresser is pretty ugly so I doubt I'd get more than like ten bucks for it," Alice responded.

"Stop messing around, I'm serious."

"What, you mean you don't even know what you're going to say to the Dean, in the unlikely chance we, like, actually get to meet with him?"

"I figured you'd think of something," Mia confessed.

"What were you going to tell him before you texted me?"

"I don't know. Maybe shoot him a few compliments. You know, boost his ego a bit. Flirt, basically."

"Mia, he's the Dean. Number one, he probably already has a high enough ego as it is. Number two, you look, like, frumpy as hell and you don't have any make-up on."

"Yeah, 'cause I don't need to pile on Mount Everest's worth of make-up to look half decent, unlike some *other* freshman in Pistachio Hall."

"I'm not the one walking around campus with colonies of bugs gestating in my hair," Alice said.

"I didn't have time this morning, and I was all worried about getting kicked out of Ingleton, and now look, I was right!"

They approached the guards and Mia put on a phony smile. "Hi guys . . . Miss me yet?"

"Are you with an escort?"

"Yes, here she is." Mia placed a hand on Alice's shoulder.

"Hey, who you calling an escort?"

Mia gave her a cold glance. "Shut up, don't cause problems for me, Alice," she muttered under her breath.

"This is my roommate, Private Cobra."

"Ex-roommate," Alice corrected.

"I just want to talk to the Dean so I can get back into Pistachio Hall. And go take my midterms tomorrow like none of this ever happened."

The guards snickered a bit, but after one of them examined the student database on his smartphone, he brandished a thumbs up. The door opened.

"Good luck," the guard said.

Mia and Alice passed through the doorway. On the other side they found an elevator.

"What am I gonna do if this doesn't work?" Mia said, more to herself than to Alice.

"Well, I guess now you can take on more hours at the coffee shop."

"Alice, you're not making me feel better."

"Just joking around. You're too serious," Alice said.

"I need you to be sympathetic."

"C'mon, you know I'm just teasing. I'm your best friend, Mia."

"Thanks, Alice . . . I knew I could count on you."

"You mean so much to me. How else would the floor get mopped at work? I sure as hell ain't doin' it," Alice said.

"I hate you."

"I hate you too."

Ding!

The twentieth floor.

They stepped cautiously into the hallway. There were men and women bustling back and forth, dressed sharply in suits and engrossed in their smartphones.

"Excuse me," Mia asked a woman in a gray suit and heels. "Do you know where we can find the Dean?"

"Are you on the Dean's schedule?" the woman asked doubtfully.

"Yeah. I have a—" Mia grabbed Alice's wrist and checked the time. "One o'clock."

"Down the hall. Room 100."

"Thanks."

The door was slightly ajar. "I'm nervous," Mia said.

"Here," Alice replied, pulling a flask out of her backpack. "Courage juice."

"Is that whiskey?"

"Sure is."

Mia took a swig with a trembling hand and handed the flask back to Alice.

Mia knocked on the door timidly. She figured she'd try flirting with the Dean.

"Who is it?" bellowed a voice. A woman's voice.

"My name's Private Sparrow. I'm a student."

"Come on in."

Mia opened the door cautiously.

Alice stayed safely at a distance, not budging an inch.

"Come on," Mia whispered to her.

"No thanks. You're going in by yourself," Alice said.

"Fine."

She stepped inside.

The room was made completely of glass (including both the ceiling and floor), which Mia concluded must have been one-way glass or else it would not have been opaque black on the outside. In the middle of the room was a desk made of expensive-looking wood. A gold statue of a penguin stood in one corner facing Mia.

The woman was seated, her back turned to Mia. All she could see was a plume of smoke and a cigar in the woman's hand, which was poking out one end of the unnecessarily tall chair.

"You're Private Sparrow," she stated.

"That's right."

"You were expelled this morning."

"That's what I'm here to talk to you about," Mia said. "I'd like to speak with the Dean."

"You're already speaking with her."

Mia assumed the Dean was a man. She didn't know what to say.

"Do you know why you were expelled?" she asked Mia.

"Was it the demerits I got in Stealth yesterday?"

"That's not the reason, Sparrow."

"Oh." A ray of hope. Some misunder-standing, perhaps?

"Let me ask you this, Private Sparrow. Do you want to be a secret agent?"

"Yes," Mia said definitively.

"Why?"

"I want to catch bad guys."

"For fun? Or because you really want to bring them to justice?"

"Well, to be honest, I think it's the fun."

"If you just want to have fun all the time, this profession is not for you," she said.

"But I like having fun. And if you have fun and get paid doing it, isn't that a sign that you've made the right career choice?"

She sighed. "Private Sparrow, you were expelled because it has been brought to my attention that you have been dating a code seven target. The guy you've been calling 'Jason.' "

Mia gulped.

"Jason must die."

"It was Alice, wasn't it? She must have blabbed." Alice and her big mouth . . . Mia was going to strangle her at the first chance she got.

"Private Sparrow, did you really think you could keep a secret like that from the

Agency? You're just a student. This is the most sophisticated organization in the entire world. We know everything about everyone. We've been monitoring your text messages with him."

"Oh . . ." Mia felt violated and sick to her stomach.

"I'm sorry, Private Sparrow, but you have to give up all of your privacy if you want to become an agent."

"Well . . ."

"You need to decide what you want. Do you want to have fun, or do you want to catch bad guys?"

"That depends . . . What do I get to do to them once I catch them?"

"Maybe this isn't for you. It's nothing to be ashamed of if it isn't."

"But no, my father would be so disappointed in me. I have to become an agent. A Black Penguin, just like him."

"Are you doing it for him, or are you doing it because you truly want it?"

"I don't know. I mean, I like joking around with my roommate," she confessed.

"And drinking—*underage*—I might add."

"Who, me?" Mia said.

She got up from the chair and faced Mia.

"You?" Mia was very confused. She thought it was a prank or something.

"Not what you expected?" It was Pablo's friend, Bonnie, dressed in a black suit. The redhead who claimed to be from Ireland.

"My name's Vulture. Agent Vulture."

"I thought you were a student," Mia said.

"A good secret agent is a master of disguise," she replied.

"But, but . . . How?"

"I know everything about you, Sparrow. Everything . . . Maybe it's time you faced the facts. This is just who you are."

"What's that supposed to mean?"

"If drinking is more important to you than your goals, then don't waste your time pursuing something that you don't care about."

"But, but . . ."

She definitely loved to drink and party. She loved it very much.

"No," she said firmly.

"No what?"

"No, I can change."

"You've said that before. Pack up, *Mia*. 'Sparrow' is going back into the codename bank."

"This time I mean it," she said with tears running down her cheeks.

She turned her back to Mia and crossed her arms. "You're dismissed. I want you out of your dorm room by Monday morning."

"I'd do anything," Mia pleaded.

"Sure you would," Vulture replied, a half-chuckle of disbelief in her tone.

"Yes. I'll give up the thing that I love most in the world."

"What's that?" Vulture asked.

"My roommate," Mia said reflexively, but instantly regretted it.

She turned to face Mia and jeered. "Please, Mia, your roommate doesn't matter to you. In fact, *nothing* really matters to you, does it?"

"Alice and I are like this." She crossed her fingers.

"You depend on her?"

"All the time. She's my best friend. We're inseparable."

"The more you depend on people, the less you achieve on your own."

She let that statement sink in. *No, it's not true*, she thought.

"Tell you what, Sparrow. You can come back if you find a new roommate."

Mia wondered if Vulture knew the two of them worked together at Sugar Dreams.

"Alice is like . . . all that I've got," Mia said.

"It's either fun, or the Agency."

"I don't know . . ."

"Time to make a choice, Private Sparrow. That is, if you want to be Agent Sparrow someday. You've got Penguin blood in you. What a waste to see you squander it. Some of the other students here would give anything to get transcripted. But you'd rather throw it all away like an idiot."

Mia's brain was tangled and she didn't have a pencil and paper to come up with a pros and cons list like she usually did when agonizing over decisions.

While she pondered the proposition, she noticed a photograph propped up on Vulture's desk. It surely must have been her husband and two kids playing at the beach.

Mia grabbed the photo off the desk.

"Your husband?" she asked.

"Four years now."

Mia did the math in her head and started to wonder how old she was. She didn't look old back at the bar. Dressed formally, she looked so different.

"Is he an agent, too?"

"We're both agents."

She looked at the kids. One boy. One girl.

Mia had always kind of assumed having kids and building a career were mutually exclusive decisions. That's what she learned from her mother.

"I see . . ." It occurred to Mia that Agent Vulture must have started her family while she was still a Private . . . Maybe even as a freshman like her.

Vulture took the photo from her hands and placed it neatly back in its proper place.

"Raising the kids is just as important as bringing criminals to justice."

Mia thought of her mother. Some part of her wanted to have kids someday. Some distant, responsible, future version of herself. But another part of her wanted to have a legacy like her father. What if generations later, people read about Agent Sparrow as required coursework in Target History 20A? Mia did not want to reach a point in her life where she had nothing to show for it except for a couple of kids.

She reached into her jeans pocket and pulled out her phone.

"Let me send out a text."

She inhaled deeply.

She typed a message to Lisa:

Looking for a new roommate.

Interested?

She hit "send."

Mia shoved the phone into her jeans pocket.

"Fun's up," Mia said. "I want to catch bad guys."

"And why do you want to? Because you want to make America proud?" Vulture took a step closer.

"No," Mia replied sternly.

"Because you want to make your father proud?"

"No."

"Why then?"

"Because I want to make myself proud."

Mia flicked a tear off her eye.

"For once."

Epilogue

MIA and Alice watched *Game of Thrones* on the couch together. Mia's move-out date was to be no later than Monday morning.

"I'm going to miss you," Mia blurted.

Alice poured two shots of Jack Daniel's.

"We'll always be friends," she said.

Mia thought about maybe texting Pablo. Just to see what he was up to. Not that she liked him or anything.

Mia's phone buzzed. A text from Jason.

Hey. Son of a bitch got away

She replied:

You asshole! Didn't u get my texts? I could have been killed!

Check the news

She opened Yahoo! and read the headline, noting the bolded caption:

"Presidential Assassination Attempt Failed, Suspect at Large."

Jason I'm breaking up with u!!!!!!

??? What are you talking about? Since when were we even dating?

I'm going to kill u!

She scrolled through menus, blocked his contact number, and threw her phone against the wall, shattering the screen.

"Oh my God, Mia! Look at your phone!"

Mia grabbed a shot glass, gulped quickly, then slammed it on the table face-down.

"Who are you texting?" Alice giggled.

"A dead guy," Mia said without remorse.

"God, Mia, you're such a flirt!"

"Yeah . . . If flirts could kill."

About the Author

Joey Young is a guy who lives in Northern California. He likes people who are weird and he has a very big bookcase. He gets his ideas from his highly bizarre brain. You can find Joey at his website at JoeyFiction.com, where he writes book reviews.

Special thanks to my two brothers, my friends, and my beloved beta readers.